For Matilda, who could easily tackle a tiger!
– S.S.

For Guy and Yves, my dearest, magical uncles
– J.D.

tiger tales
5 River Road, Suite 128, Wilton, CT 06897
Published in the United States 2023
Published in Great Britain 2022
First published in Spain 2021
by Little Tiger Press Ltd.
Text copyright © 2021 Steve Smallman
Illustrations copyright © 2021 Joëlle Dreidemy
ISBN-13: 978-1-6643-0022-4
ISBN-10: 1-6643-0022-8
Printed in China
LTP/1400/4864/0722

www.tigertalesbooks.com

THE TIGER WHO CAME FOR DINNER

by STEVE SMALLMAN

Illustrated by JOËLLE DREIDEMY

tiger tales

In a cottage deep in the woods lived Wolf, Little Lamb, and their alligator, Omelet.

They were an unusual family, but then the best families often are.

Every day they went for a walk, and every day they played their favorite game.

Morning!

FETCH!

Sometimes Omelet brought back the same stick.

Good boy, Omelet!

Sometimes he brought back a different stick.

Good try, Omelet!

And sometimes he brought back things that weren't sticks at all!

Good grief, Omelet!

One day he brought back . . .

...a little wet tiger.

"Ooh! Hello, Fluffy!" cried Little Lamb, giving the soggy tiger a great big hug. "Can we keep her, Wolf?"

Wolf shook his head. "I'm sorry, Little Lamb, but this little tiger's family must live somewhere along the river. We have to take her home."

So the next day, that's exactly what they did.
"We're going on a tiger hunt . . . ." Wolf whistled
a happy tune as they walked next to the river.

That tiger is so CUTE!

So sweet!

Everyone they met thought Fluffy was adorable!
And she was. She was cuddling Little Lamb tightly, sniffing
and snuffling behind her ear.

"That tickles!" giggled Little Lamb. "Look, Wolf, Fluffy loves me!"
But Omelet wasn't so sure.
Especially when . . .

. . . they met some mice playing tag. "Can we play?" asked Little Lamb. "Fluffy loves the mice!"

"Grrr!" said Omelet.
Fluffy loved them a little too much!
She didn't want to let them go.

"Look at the fish jumping, Fluffy!" laughed Wolf. Fluffy jumped, too. "She loves the fish!" laughed Little Lamb. But no one saw what Omelet saw!

"GRRR!" he growled, flashing his teeth. So Fluffy dropped the fish back into the water.

"That tiger is ADORABLE!" chattered a squirrel.

"Yes," agreed Wolf, "and she loves everybody! Especially Little Lamb."

"Fluffy is kissing me!" giggled Little Lamb. Omelet wasn't happy, and no one could understand why.

That tiger is SOOOO CUTE!

"Come on, Omelet," smiled Wolf. "Let's play fetch."
And in no time at all, Omelet was happy again.

Later, as the sun began to set, Wolf found a spot to put up the tent.

"Dinnertime!" he called. "Who wants carrot soup?"
"Yummy," said Little Lamb.
"Slurp!" agreed Omelet.

But Fluffy was already chewing on something . . .
Little Lamb!

"OUCH!" cried Little Lamb.

SNAP, SNAP, SNAP! went Omelet's teeth
toward Fluffy's furry tail.

"WAAAAHHHH!" cried the little tiger, bursting into tears.
"Oh, my goodness," said Wolf. "I think everyone is tired and
hungry. Let's all apologize and have a group hug."

The tiger was still crying a little bit.

But Omelet
knew better.

And while the others drifted off to sleep,
Omelet kept one eye open, all night long.

The next day, they hadn't gone
far when they saw a cottage.
"What a view!" cried Wolf.
"Is this your home, Fluffy?"

The little tiger grinned and
nodded. Then she picked up a
stick and threw it into the river!

Omelet leaped in, grabbed it, and disappeared over the waterfall's edge!

"What did you do that for, Fluffy?" gasped Wolf. "How could you?"

COME BACK!

"This is why!" snarled the little tiger. "MOM, DAD, I'M HOME! AND I'VE BROUGHT . . . DINNER!"

Two hungry-looking tigers came running out of the cottage.

"Leave her alone!" cried Wolf, holding Little Lamb tightly.
"Don't worry about him," sneered the tiger cub.
"He's a big softy."

The tigers grinned and licked their whiskers.
Closer and closer they crept, and were just
about to pounce when . . .

. . . out of the river leaped Omelet! With a very large stick clamped in his very large teeth!

CRUNCH,

CREAK,

SNAP!

went the stick.

"AAAAAAAAAAAAAAAHHHHH!"
cried the tigers.

They grabbed the tiger cub and raced into their cottage,
shutting the door with a BANG!

Wolf and Little Lamb gave the soggy alligator a g̶
"Can we go home now?" asked Little Lamb.
"Yes, let's go home," agreed Wolf.
So back down the mountain went Wolf and Little Lamb
with Omelet. He wasn't small or cute—and he would never
be fluffy—but he was family, and they loved him.